My Dear Children,

Before you read *To the Ends of the Earth*, I would like to tell you the backstory. You see, the backstory is the story that happened back before there was a story at all.

The Backstory of To the Ends of the Earth

Last fall, a raging fire burned hundreds of acres of the forest near my home. Now it is spring, and I am working with a group of volunteers to help clear the fallen trees from the hiking trails that weave through the hills and canyons I love so much.

Knowing that fire is a healthy and essential part of a forest's life cycle doesn't take away the sadness I feel seeing the blackened remains. But even as we work, deep beneath the surface, life is already beginning, as it has for thousands of years.

Although they couldn't have known when the fire was coming, lodgepole pine trees know that someday there will be a fire. To make sure new trees will grow after a fire, they produce some pinecones sealed with a thick resin that keep the seeds safe inside. During a fire, when temperatures reach nearly 400°, the sticky resin melts, and the seeds are released into the ground, where a new generation of trees will take root.

The charcoaled remains of the burned trees will also help the forest to make a new start. The charcoal provides phosphorous and potassium, needed by the plants as they begin to grow. After a few weeks of sunny days and spring showers, this burn area will dance with tender sprouts of grass and colorful wildflowers—a joyous sign that the forest eco-system continues to thrive.

As hikers return, they will hear woodpeckers pecking for bugs in the burned tree trunks. And, if they watch quietly, they will see rabbits and other small critters who stayed safe from the fire in their underground burrows. They may even be lucky enough to spy a mule deer with her fawn enjoying the freshly sprouted grass.

After a long day working we gathered around the campfire. With the Milky Way stretching above us, the conversation faded until the only sounds were the crackling of the fire and a Pygmy-Owl hooting in the distance. Young and old, short and tall—strangers this morning, we had become friends, bound together by our love of the forest. And we were exhausted.

One by one, each volunteer headed off to the tents, leaving Buddy, my border collie, and me to enjoy the crisp cool evening. Buddy knows nothing of forest fires but loves to come along and spend the day cheering me on. As I petted his soft fur,

Buddy's ears suddenly perked up, and his head jerked around toward the darkness.

Moving cautiously, a little boy with tears rolling down his cheeks stepped out of the shadows. There were no children with our group. So, I was quite surprised to see this young boy.

Slowly, he inched closer and between sobs, told me his name was Hayden. He was lost and afraid his mother would never find him. He had seen our campfire and was hoping she was here.

Calming his fears, I told him we had not seen her but was sure she would find him soon. Then I asked him to stay with us because when you are lost in the forest, you should stay in one place until you are found. As he sat by the fire, I woke the head volunteer to call the forest service to report the lost boy.

Hayden snuggled up to Buddy and happily poked at the fire with a long stick as we waited. I leaned against a blackened stump, and looking up into the sparkling sky, I saw a shooting star—a sign of good luck. I knew his mother would come.

While we were watching the moon rise there was a noise in the forest. We heard a branch break, and then someone called out, "H A Y D E N! H A Y D E N!"

From the other side of a huge rock, the little boy's mother and a forest service guide appeared. With joyous laughter, Hayden ran to her as fast as his legs could go. Jumping into her arms, he told her how afraid he had been that she would never find him.

Holding Hayden tightly, she sat down by the fire and told him a story of how she would go to the ends of the earth for him. She would fly across the ocean, climb the highest mountain, and hike through the darkest jungle to find him, to keep him safe, or just to see him smile.

As I watched him melt into his mother's arms, I realized the story she told is what we all wish for—someone who will go to the ends of the earth for us.

Turn the page to begin the story that honors Hayden, his mother Lucy, and all the others who have a love so strong they will tirelessly journey *To the Ends of the Earth*.

This book is dedicated to
my Jessica Lynn, who inspired this story
and a love that has grown from the very first day.

To Jessie, Carrie, and Johnny, whom I carry in my heart,
knowing our paths will merge ahead—perhaps today.

And to those on love's journey—
remember, there are no maps.
But trust in love, and it will guide you
to the ends of the earth and back.

To The Ends of the Earth

By Sharon Thayer

Illustrations by Reuben McHugh
and Andrew Smith

Before you came into my world,
I knew I'd love a boy or girl.

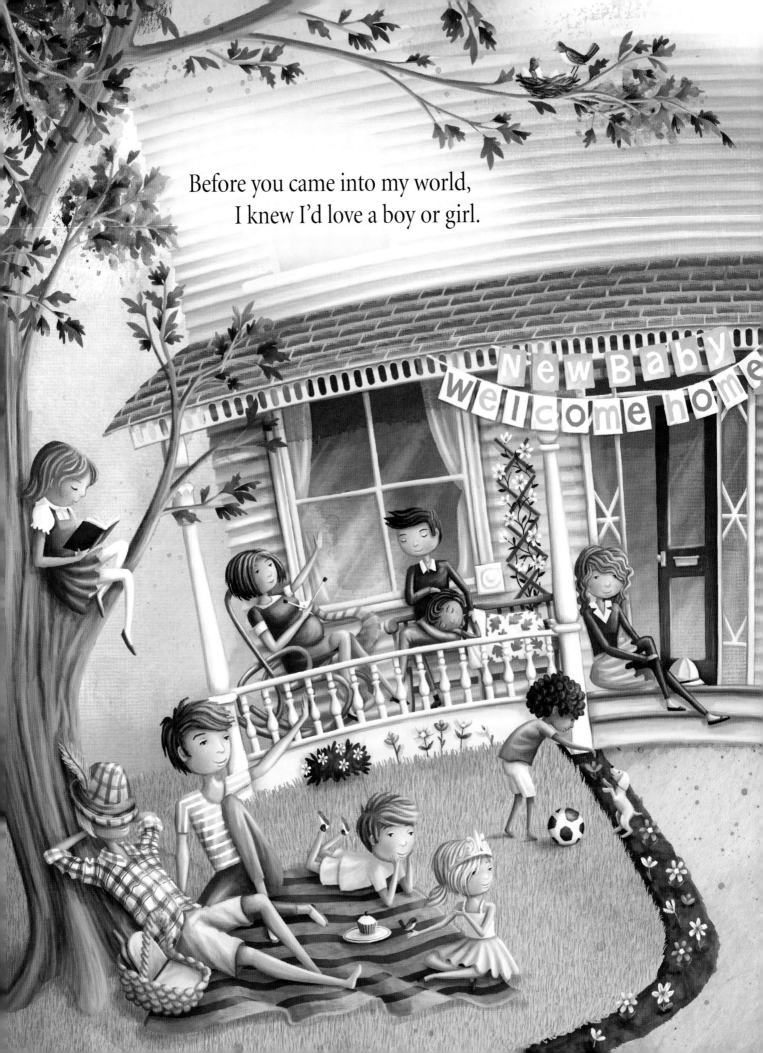

But the first time I held you, I knew,
I'd go to the
ends of the earth for you!

If you were sad and lost your smile,
I'd plan to cheer you for a while.
We'd cross the sea on a red macaw,
flying high to the plains of Africa.

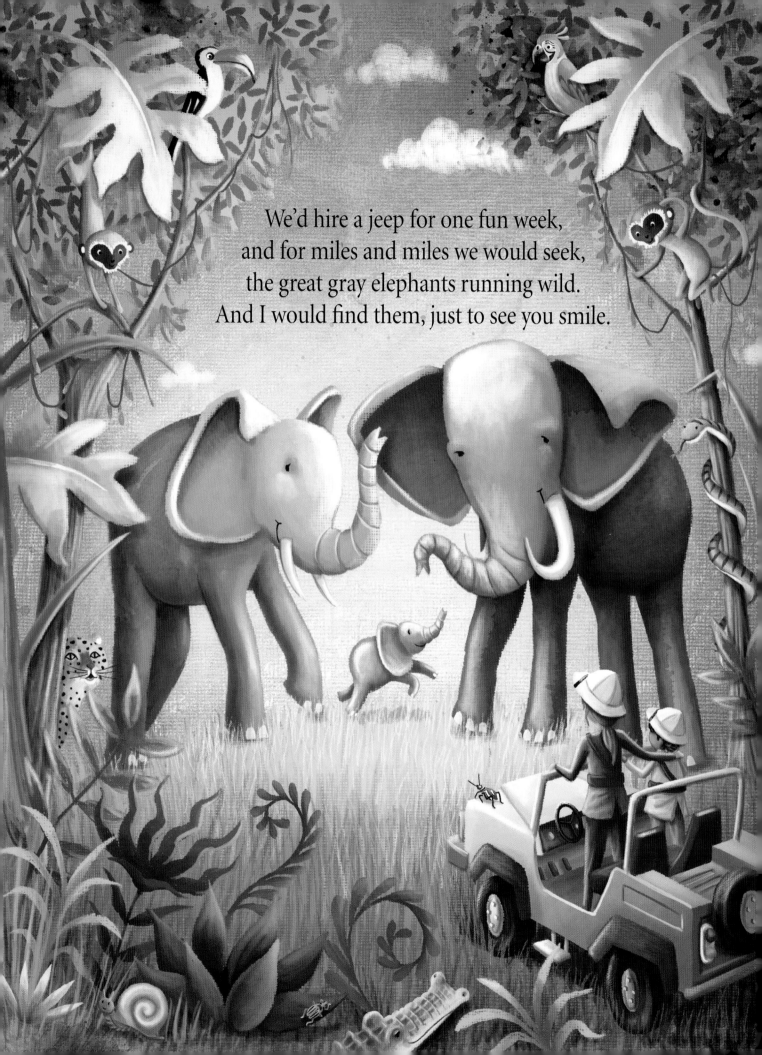

We'd hire a jeep for one fun week,
and for miles and miles we would seek,
the great gray elephants running wild.
And I would find them, just to see you smile.

If you were scared clear through the night,
I'd stay with you and hold you tight.
The very next day, we'd sail away,
to find a warrior so strong and so brave.

He'd have a bone right through his nose,
and hair so long, it'd touch his toes!
His mask would look quite scary to you,
until you saw his kind eyes shining through.

Much stronger than a hurricane,
and fast as lightning in the rain,
at home with us, he'd guard your door,
so you would never be scared anymore.

If you were bored one lonely day,
we'd make a plan and get away.
To the vast Black Forest we would go,
clip-clopping along through the cold and snow.

We'd find the man with just one leg, who'd build a clock with cogs and pegs.
It'd strike each hour, and into view,
would come fine ladies and gentlemen, too.

The chimes would sound as they danced about,
and then that bird would start to shout.
He'd cuckoo once, for every hour,
then cuckoo again, and more, and more,
'til you fell laughing on the floor.

If your pink tongue began to swell,
I'd find a cure to make you well.
Through forests and over mountain tops,
through blizzards and storms, I would not stop,

until I found the lovely witch,
who brews up potions for the sick.

She'd mix a drink you would not like,
with herbs and oils and stars of night.

Then touch your cheeks
and kiss your brow,
and magically, you'd be healed somehow.

If you were tired and had no bed,
to the Amazon River I'd head,
to hunt for patches of rare green moss,
to stuff in a mattress, fluffy and soft.

I'd gather clouds and rays of sun,
and weave a blanket, second-to-none.

And then, I'd pick bright flowers of spring,
to fill a pillow of butterfly wings.

Sweet scents would dance around your head,
as you lay cozy in your bed.
Soon angels, floating on the breeze,
would gather 'round and sing you to sleep.

If you began to frown again,
I'd find a rainbow for you, and then,
I'd knit the colors into scarves and hats.
Who wouldn't line up for clothes like that?

The line would grow throughout the day,
and soon become a grand parade.
A fancy penguin would lead the way,
then giraffes and zebras who'd strut and sway.

Six monkeys would come from Belize,
and do exactly as they please,
while high above, great birds would glide,
leading us on to where you reside.

You'd spy a unicorn on the run,
then leap on her back to join the fun.

Together, we'd march around the town,
up streets and down, until you'd lost your frown.

If you were cold, to make you warm,
I'd ask the bees all in a swarm,
to fly us high until we'd find,
the floating Kingdom of Fire and Light.

As we would tiptoe in between,
while searching for the King and Queen,
each flame would give a gift of heat,
to warm you up, from your head to your feet.

All night we'd dance in misty swirls,
with all the royals of this world.

We'd make a memory to warm your nights,
when I'm not there and the world's not right.

I'd go to the ends of the earth for you,
and do these things, it's certainly true.
But there are no ends of our great earth.
No beginnings or ends for which to search.
It turns forever, 'round and 'round,
just like the special
love we've found.

Around and around
as your story unwinds,
wherever life takes you,
whatever life makes you,
I will love you, like the very first time.

Each time I see a shooting star, I imagine Hayden and his mother, flying off to the ends of the earth on the back of a great bird. That makes me think about the people I see every day sharing all sorts of love: parent and grandparent love, forever partnerships, friendships, love of animals and nature, and the love of adventure.

Then, I start to dream about my next adventure. About the distances I will travel to find another story to entertain you. I hope to see you out there too, hiking and biking along the trails as you travel to the ends of the earth for the loves of your life.

As always, remember to go outside and explore, because you never know what you might find on the other side of the door.

Never stop believing!

Ms. Sharon

To The Ends of the Earth

First edition 2019
10 9 8 7 6 5 4 3 2

Layout & Graphics - Jenny Hancey, Jenny@HanceyDesign.com
Editing - Sharon Roe, Sharon@SharonRoe.com

Carousel Publishing
5061 Pine Cone Lane • Tyler, TX 75707
903-871-9872
sharon@Carousel-Publishing.com
www.Carousel-Publishing.com

Library of Congress Cataloging-in-Publication Data
Thayer, Sharon C.

Summary: A lyrical "love story" that illustrates how far one will go to keep their little ones safe
and happy. At some point, all children get bored, sick, upset, or afraid. When that happens, it's
important to know they have someone who will, literally, go to the ends of the earth for them.

1. Love juvenile fiction 2. New baby juvenile fiction
3. Parental love juvenile fiction 4. Valentine's Day juvenile fiction

ISBN: 978-0-9766239-9-1
LCCN: 2019909867

Printed in the United States.
FSC certified paper to promote sustainable forestry.

Carousel
PUBLISHING